Produced by Kroha Associates, Inc.
Middletown, Connecticut.

Printed in the United States of America.

ISBN 1-56326-111-1

# I Want To Win

By Ruth Lerner Perle

One day, Minnie, Daisy, Lilly, and Clarabelle were having lunch in the school cafeteria when they overheard the softball coach talking.

"Did you hear that!" Minnie cried. "There's room for one more player on the school softball team, and the tryouts are next week! I always wanted to be on the softball team."

"The tryout is made up of four parts — throwing a ball, catching, batting, and running," Lilly said. "Whoever does the best gets to be on the team."

"That won't be easy," Clarabelle said.

"I bet I can make the team," Minnie said. "I'm a pretty good softball player. The only one who could beat me is you, Daisy." Minnie turned to Daisy and said, "You wouldn't try out if I did, would you?"

"Well, I'd like to be on the team too, Minnie, so I guess I *will* try out," Daisy said.

The next day, Minnie put on her pink jogging suit and her favorite hightop sneakers, and went to the school track to practice running. Penny, Clarabelle, and Lilly came to watch.

As Minnie made her first trip around the track, she saw someone running toward her. It was Daisy! As they passed, Minnie noticed that Daisy was wearing a pink jogging suit and hightop sneakers just like hers.

Daisy waved to her friends. "Hi, everybody! Watch how fast I can run!" she called.

*I'm going to try really hard to do better than Daisy at the tryouts,* Minnie thought to herself.

Early the next day, Minnie practiced throwing a softball. Lilly, Clarabelle, and Penny took turns catching as Minnie threw the ball to them.

Then Daisy practiced throwing a softball and the three girls took turns helping *her*.

Minnie watched as Daisy threw the ball. *Daisy's really good!* Minnie thought.

Later, Minnie went to the park and practiced catching. She used her favorite glove for good luck and caught all the balls her friends threw to her.

Before long, Daisy came to the park too, and the girls helped her practice her catching. Minnie watched from nearby.

The next day, Minnie practiced her batting.

So did Daisy. Minnie watched Daisy out of the corner of her eye and saw that Daisy was a very good player. Minnie was getting more and more worried. And the more worried she became, the more upset she was that Daisy was trying out for the team.

Penny, Clarabelle, and Lilly didn't know what to do.

"The tryouts are tomorrow morning," Lilly said. "Minnie and Daisy are both our friends. Which one shall we root for?"

At last it was the day of the tryouts. The coach welcomed everybody and said, "I know all of you have been working hard all week. There's only one spot open on our team, so do your best, and may the best player win."

Minnie's heart was pounding. She looked over at her friends. She wondered what Daisy was thinking.

The first test was throwing a ball at a target. Each girl had five chances.

Minnie aimed carefully and threw the ball. She hit the target three times.

"Hooray!" her friends shouted.

When it was Daisy's turn, she took careful aim and hit the target four times.

"Hooray!" the girls shouted.

The coach announced: "3 for Minnie, 4 for Daisy."

The next part was catching a ball.
Minnie caught the ball four out of five times.
The coach announced the total: "7 for Minnie, 4 for Daisy."
Both girls were doing very well. None of the other players had even come close to their scores.

When it was Daisy's turn to catch, she caught the ball three out of five times.

"The score is even," the coach declared. "Minnie has seven points and Daisy has seven."

The batting tryouts came next.

Crack! Crack! Crack! Crack! Crack! Both Minnie and Daisy hit the ball five out of five times.

Everyone jumped to their feet and cheered.

The coach quieted the crowd. "The score is tied," he announced. "There is just one final event — the running race. The winner of the race will be on the team."

Daisy and Minnie took their places at the starting line. Minnie could feel herself getting more and more nervous.

"Ready," said the coach, "get set" — then he blew the starting whistle.

Minnie and Daisy started running as fast as they could.
First Daisy was ahead,
     then Minnie,
          then Daisy,
               then Minnie.

By the last stretch Daisy was getting out of breath and had to slow down. Minnie was tired too, but she kept on running and thinking to herself, *I want to win, I want to win*.

She ran and ran, and was the first one to cross the finish line.

Everybody clapped and shouted.

"Congratulations, Minnie!" the coach said. "You are the winner — and the newest member of our school softball team!"

Then he added, "Congratulations also go to Daisy for being a good competitor and a good sport. It sure was a close race."

Minnie sat with Daisy on the bench. "I feel funny," Minnie told her. "I'm glad I won, but I'm sorry you lost."

Then Daisy looked up at Minnie and said, "I feel funny, too. I'm sorry I lost, but I'm glad you won."

Daisy shook Minnie's hand and said, "Congratulations, Minnie. I tried my best, but you won fair and square. You're the lucky winner!"

Minnie smiled. "You're right, Daisy. I *am* lucky, but it's because I have a friend like you," she said.

Daisy was a really good sport that day! Did you ever compete with a friend? Did you win or lose?